The Village of

Little Comely-on-the-Marsh

The Village of Little Comely-on-the-Marsh

Alan L. Simons

BARONEL BOOKS
Toronto

The Village of Little Comely-on-the-Marsh is about diversity, cultural and religious issues, to name but a few, in today's society.

The hilarious story weaves around the lives of an eccentric Welsh community living in a small village somewhere in the south of France exclusively in their own sheltered world.

The book facetiously addresses concerns that go beyond the stereotypes of British and French society. Written with humour and a romantic slant, it demonstrates that we are all equal, irrespective of where we come from.

Pre-release Reviews

"Alan L. Simons is a brilliant writer of romantic and humorous fiction with fascinating characters and myriad insights into human nature. It seizes readers gently by the throat and does not release until the final scene. Having lived in France, I think he catches much about its people and culture too."

-David Kilgour, Ottawa. Author of several non-fiction books.

"A most compelling erudite novella was experienced by this reviewer. This work transcends an analysis of contemporary ethnocentric morality and behaviour… The imagery used and metamorphic insightful exposition compels one to read this volume numerous times. Attempts to analyze and correct normative and deviant national and individual behaviour replete as it were in the "Welsh and Usman" ethnicities and dialects are outstanding. Suffice to say a work with a timeless contribution to the literate and open minded."

- Dr Samuel Sussman RAMI, Vancouver BC

"This is a fascinating story, beautifully written, so much so that one can imagine the village actually existing. The characters involved are truly believable. The story keeps you gripped to carry on reading, discovering the diversity of the villagers, as the undertones come to the surface."

- L- j. T. West Berkshire U.K

"A heart-warming, whimsical and inspirational tale set in a fun village with charming and eccentric characters. A must read from Alan L. Simons, truly a mischievous writer with a wonderful imagination."

-*David Eisenstadt, Toronto, ON*

"If you enjoy British humour, you'll love *The Village of Little Comely-on-the-Marsh*, the latest novel by Alan L. Simons. One of the appealing features of Simons' writing is his tongue-in-cheek writing style—for example, the clever way he juxtaposes multiple languages from time to time. It's a quick read—you can't wait for the sequel. In fact, *The Village of Little Comely-on-the-Marsh* is so graphic in nature that it almost cries out to become a movie or a television series."

--*Rabbi Corinne Copnick, Los Angeles, CA.*

"A delightful model of English whimsy, with a cast of oddballs, so uniquely goofy, they're each worth a story of their own. It takes awhile for the plot to take off, but who cares, the persona are so appealing. Great as read aloud or inspired improvisation."

-*Ralph Wintrob. Teacher-Librarian, Toronto, ON*

"True humour springs not more from the head than from the heart. It is not contempt; its essence is love. It issues not in laughter, but in still smiles, which lie far deeper."

-Thomas Carlyle

.The Village of Little Comely-on-the-Marsh
Alan L. Simons

This is a work of fiction. Any resemblance between the names, characters and localities stated in this book and any persons, living or dead, is purely coincidental and possibly due to the reader's vivid imagination.

The moral right of the author has been asserted.

Contact the author at baronelbooks@gmail.com

The Village of Little Comely-on-the-Marsh has its own website.
https://comelyonthemarsh.wordpress.com

ISBN: 978-0-9877503-7-2

To my wonderful family, who continue to have the patience to put up with my unique sense of humour and style.

.

Acknowledgements

I gratefully acknowledge OdeK for her counsel in the design of the book's front cover and to LT for her constructive advice in the characterisations mentioned in this book.

Shamelessly, I have used a number of quotes in the book taken from various sources, including *BrainyQuote*, the world's largest quotation site.

The Village of
Little Comely-on-the Marsh

ABOUT 20 kilometres from Luc-en-Diois, on the river Drôme, and about 11 kilometres from La Motte-Chalançon, located in the department Drôme, in the south of France, somewhere lies the Village of Little Comely-on-the-Marsh.

You won't find Little Comely-on-the-Marsh located on any map. Nor will you find any reference to it in any of the libraries in Valence or Gap. If you asked the residents of Luc-en-Diois or La Motte-Chalançon about it, they probably would deny its existence, mumbling under their breath: *"Va te faire cuire un oeuf!"* (Go suck an egg!)

You see, for all intent and purposes, Little Comely-on-the-Marsh is, well, in the wrong place. It shouldn't even exist.

No one knows for sure how the village acquired its name, or from where its 347 Welsh inhabitants, plus 115 cats, 143 dogs, one horse, two pigs, a milking cow and four sheep came. It seems there were some stories about the Romans bringing the Welsh over in the 5th Century to tend their sheep. After a few centuries, they became bored with the area. They left having dismissed the local French wineries of the time as, *"Urinae et a cattus est melior!"* (The urine of a cat is better!) But this was just hearsay, handed down from century to century by the villagers. There it was.

Of course today, the French being 'the French' blamed it on a British Brexit imperial conspiracy to take over yet another part of their country and anglicise it. However, confusion reigned, and rumours abound. None of which came to any fruition.

None of Little Comely-on-the Marsh's 347 Welsh inhabitants spoke French or wanted to for that matter. They're an odd bunch; eccentric is a word that comes to mind. Simply put, they had an islander mentality in the middle of rural southern France, keeping to themselves in seclusion for literally hundreds of years.

It was rare for any 'bloody foreigner', so put by its inhabitants, to find the place. Even throughout the many wars fought on French soil, Little Comely-on-the-Marsh seemed to have missed all the action. Wars came and went; major world disasters appeared out of nowhere; men landed on the moon; the warming of the planet; France won the World Cup in 1998, and then there was COVID-19. Strangely, none seem to affect the village.

The citizens of Little Comely-on-the-Marsh voted years ago not to have anything to do with TV. After all, it was French, wasn't it- and as far as telephones, only one existed in the village just outside the pub, and mobiles – forget it! For they were a sheer menace to their way of life.

Surrounding the village pond stood three primary buildings. The pub, naturally called, The Duke of

Wellington faced the pond on the sunny side.

Directly opposite, an upscale restaurant called Welcome Restaurant and Tea Rooms and thirdly, what would a Welsh village be without its fish and chip shop, which also doubled-up as the butchers, dentist and barbershop.

It would be fair to say that 'Little Comely', as its inhabitants know it, is more Welsh than the Welsh. A bastion, of the Welsh National Anthem, *"Hen Wlad Fy Nhadau"* (The Land of My Fathers). Something from another era, living up to the expectations, traditions and rituals that no longer exist in their home country. Yes, tradition played an essential part in the lives of all who lived in Little Comely-on-the-Marsh.

Little Comely-on-the-Marsh was self-sufficient in every aspect, never needing to introduce anything French into the village. No French veggies, fruit or meat for them, and indeed no French wine or potatoes, thank you very much!

So, one asks, are the inhabitants of Little Comely-on-the-Marsh, French or Welsh? Yes, of course, technically they are French. But not according to its inhabitants, who have no time for the likes of the EU, Brexit or its trade policies. And one can forget about the Euro.

Yes, those who live in Little Comely know precisely who they are. It is still pounds, shillings and pence for them, which disappeared years ago from Britain. In any case, no one had ever heard of anyone venturing into Little Comely-on-the Marsh, or expressing a wish to leave. That is, until recently.

And this is where my story begins. ☼

One typical French Sunday spring morning in Luc-en-Diois, the mist had hardly risen, and the delicious smell of the first un bol de café au lait had still to be made at Le Relais du Claps restaurant. A young man by the name of Usman took the 31-kilometre journey by car to visit his grandmother. She lived in La Motte-Chalançon. Unfortunately, en route, his car skidded on the slippery road driving around a bend and ended up in a ditch. His car was a complete write-off.

If you are cognizant of this area, you would be aware route, D61 isn't known for its abundance of vehicular traffic, and not at seven-thirty on a Sunday morning. So, the chances of either a vehicle stopping to assist Usman or for that matter, a local French farmer, out for his early morning jog before milking his one and only Montbéliarde, were not too encouraging.

Fortunately, and as typical of a young man, Usman didn't believe he was too badly hurt. He assumed no broken bones other than a few cuts, grazes, some rips in his clothing and an awful headache. He felt immensely relieved until he saw his life-blood to his world; his prize-possession mobile phone had smashed into pieces. What on earth was he supposed to do? For as any common sense adult over the age of 60 knows, no young adult can survive for more than a few minutes without their mobile phone.

Well, Usman hadn't a clue where he was, although he remembered seeing a sign saying *Establet* a few kilometres back. So, grudgingly he decided to start walking. And walk he did! Within the hour, Usman, trudging through the early morning spring rain, came across an intersection. It was decision time. No problem! He reached into his back pocket for his mobile, an automatic response as one knows that occurs hundreds of times daily in the city. But alas, now he had to think. He thought that he might consider walking straight on, or should he perhaps turn left? What direction was north? For some inexplicable reason, he turned right. He proceeded to walk in the drizzling rain, along a winding back road that led to absolutely nowhere.

Within thirty minutes, Usman started to regret his decision. He was getting cold and thirsty, and he was wet and wanted a coffee. He should have waited until *Le Relais du Claps* had opened their doors at eight-thirty. Also, the terrain had engulfed his tracks, and his head was beginning to throb even more. Usman wondered where this was all heading. Yet, perhaps just by an inner sense of something he sensed, drove him on to continue walking.

Stumbling along, feeling hungry and with a pulsing headache, he finally collapsed and sheltered under a large plane tree where he fell into a deep asleep.

Hello! And what's your name then?"

Usman awoke to find himself in a huge bed covered with starched white sheets. The pillows, two of them, flowered in a plethora of vibrant colours, smelt like his grandmother's lavender bush. He faced an open window overlooking a garden of great beauty. His head, still pulsating from the accident, had been bound up with a white, red and green bandage.

"Hello there! And what's your name? Has the cat got your tongue?"

In front of him, Usman saw two young ladies. At least he thought there were two.

"My name is Felicity, and this is my twin sister Penelope."

Usman looked at them in dismay, for he couldn't understand a word they were saying. He shrugged his shoulders, closed his eyes and fell back to sleep.

"Oh dear me," the twins said in unison. "I think

we have a foreigner amongst us."

"You better run right away and tell Mayor Hastings we have a foreigner amongst us," said Felicity to Penelope, with an air of no-nonsense authority.

Sometime later, Usman opened his eyes to find himself scrutinised by a gathering of people who were intently looking at him with curiosity and suspicion.

"Er… hum! My name is Mr Norman Hastings, Mayor of Little Comely-on-the-Marsh and this here," he said, pointing to a large rotund lady flouting a flowered hat and white gloves, "is my wife, Mildred."

Norman Hastings continued by pointing, in no particular order, to the remaining assembly of people. "Chief Constable Gruffydd." The one-eyed police officer came forward to take a good look at the foreigner in their midst while instructing his police dog Waterloo to sit still. "Dr Jacobs is our medical Doctor, coroner and pharmacist. Mr Wellesley Llewellyn is our publican and owner of

The Duke of Wellington, and this is his lovely daughter Blodwin."

The Mayor continued with a wave of his hands. "Captain Idris, our legal representative." The Mayor turned to look at the twins. "Ah, yes! You've already met our two wonderful young nurses, Felicity and Penelope," he said blushing with a smile on his face. His wife, Mildred, gave him a dirty look. He continued. "This here is Owain, our barber, dentist, butcher and abattoir owner." The Mayor turned to a little whimsical figure sitting under the window sill. "And that's my son Twm," he said with a faint-hearted sigh that everyone in the room acknowledged with a nod of their heads, whilst looking at each other as if to say, yes we know Twm is a little different.

Chief Constable Gruffydd, approached the bed, looked at the Mayor for his approval and said slowly and loudly, *"Wyt ti'n siarad Saesneg?"* (Do you speak English?)

Mayor Hastings put his hands to his face. "No, Chief Constable, whoever he is," pointing his chubby index finger directly at Usman's nose, "I doubt very much if he can speak Welsh. Goodness gracious me! Ask him again in English, please!"

"Do you speak English?"

Usman, who may have only been a small-town *mécanicien automobile* with primary education, figured out incorrectly, the Chief Constable was asking for his name. "Usman."

Chief Constable Gruffydd stepped back to address the group standing behind him. "I think he said he speaks Usman."

Entirely baffled, everyone started to talk over each other. "What on earth is an Usman?" Mildred, the Mayor's wife asked. "It's certainly not one of those peculiar French dialects, is it?" remarked Captain Idris. "It must be foreign," he added to the look of confusion on all their faces.

"Let's keep the knowledge of our visitor's presence just to ourselves for the time being," said Mayor Hastings, to which all those present nodded their heads in agreement.

Dr Jacobs stepped forward. He had one of

those expressive looks on his face that only doctors can muster when taking over a situation. "Now, now. He has to rest. He needs time. He has a nasty bump on his head, and he has a raging temperature. Felicity and Penelope will take good care of him." The twins smiled, looked at each other and nodded in a way that any intelligent person could figure out there was trouble brewing ahead! With a wave of his hand, Dr Jacobs steered everyone, other than Felicity and Penelope, out of the room.

The two girls dressed in their nurses' uniforms weren't precisely the uniforms we know today. One suspects no nurse these days in their right mind, while on duty, would wear a short tight white skirt with high heels. And both of the girls were in full competition mode to see who wore the sharpest outfit. Even in his ill state, Usman recognised this as something beneficial to his well-being.

Usman's positive thoughts abruptly came to an end as nurse Penelope pulled back his bedsheets, rolled him over with a certain amount of well-planned enthusiasm, and propelled a large thermometer up his rear end. It would seem Usman had begun, in no uncertain manner, to understand these were the ways of the Village of Little Comely-on-the-Marsh.

Over the next three days, Usman was visited by members of the Village Council comprising of Mayor Hastings and his five councillors. Captain Idris, their legal representative; Gweneth Evans, their Business Manager; Owain Jones, Transportation; Harri Thomas, Parks & Recreation, and Dafyyd Williams, Conservation, Health & Wellness.

Mayor Hastings, when his wife Mildred wasn't following his shadow, was known throughout the village as the foremost authority on learning how to speak one's mind without regard to the consequences. He was, also known by the patrons of The Duke of Wellington pub, as someone whose total knowledge of the village's practical affairs was less than zero. One word summed up Mayor Hastings. Fake! Perhaps that was the reason Chief Constable Gruffydd had the unenviable task of escorting the Mayor everywhere he went. One could question, in at least today's world, why had he been elected by the vast majority of the village's 347 people? The answer lays somewhere in the Welsh saying, *"A wyr leiag a ddwed fwyaf."* (He who knows least talks most.) For as I write these words to you, Little Comely-on-the-Marsh functioned splendidly by the blessed organisational skills of no-nonsense Gweneth Evans, the Village Business Manager extraordinaire! ☼

The Village Council met once a month on a Monday morning for two hours starting with a healthy Welsh breakfast. The Council had a strict agenda. Ninety minutes for breakfast, followed by a 30-minute discussion regarding village business. They were very specific as to the time they took over breakfast. The meal always consisted of dry-cured Welsh bacon, pork sausages, a couple of free-range eggs, fried lava cakes, and if in season, grilled tomatoes, all topped off with a Penclawdd cockle and a large pot of tea. It was a prime example of a first-class Welsh breakfast feast that certainly had no difficulty lasting for the entire allocated period.

Catered by Welcome Restaurant and Tea Rooms, the village's 3-star Michelin establishment, the meal was prepared under the direction of renowned Michelin chef Meurig ap Griffiths. He had a lineage dating back to the early Welsh kings. Regardless of the Michelin award, this in itself secured his right, by his customers, to produce the exceptional breakfast cuisine.

Now, yes you're probably wondering how on earth the Village of Little Comely-on-the-Marsh's Welcome Restaurant and Tea Rooms attained the Michelin accreditation. For it's certainly not listed in The Michelin Guide. What I can tell you is the village's size had no bearing on it. After all, there were other villages located in Europe that had acquired 3-stars. Kruiningen in the Netherlands, Brusaporto in Italy and Dries, Germany comes immediately to mind.

There is one other restaurant situated just about 194 kilometres from Little Comely in Saint-Bonnet le Froid, population 244. One's imagination might suggest somehow 15 years ago, on route D61, the Michelin logo got into the hands of Welcome's junior partner, none other than Mayor Norman Hastings. Ergo! And let's leave it like that!

Mayor Hastings was the first member of the Village Council to visit Usman. Dr Jacobs had set up a rigid visitation schedule. Ten minutes per person. One person at a time, although the rule was waived for the Mayor and Chief Constable Gruffydd.

Gruffydd initiated the questioning. "Other than telling us he speaks a language called Usman, has he spoken to you girls?" Felicity and Penelope looked at each other and shook their heads.

Dr Jacobs, a doctor of the variety known for having passionate integrity for respect and discretion, intervened. "Mayor Hastings, our young man is in no fit condition to be cross-examined and especially not by…" Dr Jacobs looked directly into Chief Constable Gruffydd's only eye. He continued: "And not by Gruffydd."

Felicity and Penelope continued with their daily chore of nursing, but they knew what Dr

Moishe Jacobs meant. The one-eyed Chief Constable Gruffydd, with the egotism of the Pharisees, wasn't disposed to anyone who didn't follow the traditions of the Welsh Methodist evangelical revival Christian faith. And now, his suspicions, with the foreigner amongst them who spoke Usman, had increased the total to two. For Gruffydd, two were two too many.

"Yes, yes, yes! I understand. Perhaps we'll return on another occasion. Come, Gruffydd, time to leave." And with that, a red-faced Mayor Hastings followed by his Chief Constable said their goodbyes.

Usman, the Usman who spoke Usman, might not have understood the language of these strange people, but he was well versed in perceiving their body language.

Usman grew up as a young boy in the Alawite village of Nahr al-Bared in north-west Syria, where his family lived on the outskirts of the village. Usman enjoyed fishing, and often he would walk to the Orontes River and gaze into the water, wondering if he would soon be strong enough to catch a barbel. But that wasn't to be. Because of the Syrian war, all his surviving family fled to Lebanon and from there to France.

It was in the refugee camp in Lebanon that he spent much of his time observing people. He concluded, quite correctly, not all Syrian refugees felt empathy towards each other.

These experiences helped him grasp what it meant to be Alawite, a minority Syrian sect who are encouraged to drink wine socially in moderation and believe in reincarnation.

From their earliest infancy, Felicity and Penelope knew they wanted to become nurses, a profession much admired by every boy reaching puberty in their school. All of the twins' appreciation for nursing was confirmed as they grew up as teenagers working part-time at the Welcome Restaurant and Tea Rooms. It was if nursing found them. Dr Jacobs was the co-conspirator. While eating a portion of his Welsh rarebit, a piece became lodged in his windpipe, and no end of coughing and trying to clear his throat would the lump go away. Sensing the emergency, the twins by instinct, hastily took up the challenge and after asking the Doctor if he was choking, taking turns, magnificently applied the Heimlich Maneuver on him.

It remains a mystery to this day how the twins knew what to do. Still, they came through like champions, to which Dr Jacobs rewarded them with their lifetime ambition, to be nurses. After studying for two years, under the supervision of Dr Jacobs, he announced they were ready to assist him in his medical practice.

Unbeknown to Usman, the twins' acclaim to nursing was only declared a few hours before he arrived at the clinic. He was affirmed as their first real live patient and Penelope, with a smile directed at her sister, decided to take control of the situation.

If there was something nurse Penelope had managed to do after her rear end faux pas, it was in her attempt to raise Usman's spirits. His rear-ending awakened him from his intergalactic journey and was immediately recognised by

Felicity and Penelope as a sign Usman had finally return to life.

"Hello, anyone here?" Captain Idris' head, could be seen between the clinic's two swinging doors. Idris was an unusual character, even by the village's standards. He was a very deaf 89-year-old court jester figure. Still, with one of the best legal minds in the village who knew everything there was to know about 12th-century Welsh law called *Cyfraith Hywel*, or Law of Howel, but little else. Sadly over time, with no clients, he became agitated and reckless, causing fits of depression, which led him to decide to make a career change. At the age of 69 years, Captain Idris self-appointed himself in the uniform of a WWI Royal Flying Corps pilot decked out with leather hat and goggles, the traditional white silk scarf and a leather jacket.

He had a companion. A friend by the name of Aelwen, She never left his side, a constant companion. But she had her faults. Aelwen, you see, was a life-size blow-up doll, dressed to kill and always attached to the Captain's left foot.

To those of you who aren't familiar with these

oddities, perhaps I ought to explain. Captain Idris was right-handed.

His interest in the village's foreigner wasn't at least of a curious nature. It was one both Felicity and Penelope saw through instantly. He had been sent by Mayor Hastings to infiltrate the clinic and conduct a soft interrogation on Usman, the Usman who spoke Usman. His companion Aelwen would act as a decoy.

Captain Idris and Aelwen were given precisely five minutes by the village's medical team to do what they were best at doing. And for the first four minutes, all three stared at each other. Usman was particularly intrigued with Aelwen. He couldn't recollect the last time he had been stared at by a blow-up doll, and certainly not one attached to a WWI pilot's left foot.

By the time Captain Idris had expressed his first utterance, "Mm, yes hello!" a comment that would have put him in the same category as, let us say, an antelope casually walking up to a hungry lion, it was time for him and Aelwen to move on to better things.

That same morning, The Welcome Restaurant and Tea Rooms sent over to Usman a perfect French breakfast. Created exclusively by chef Meurig ap Griffiths, it consisted of a sweet pastry, two freshly baked warm croissant with butter and jam, juice, yoghurt and steaming coffee, all of which was looked upon in disdain by his very Welsh nurses. But what caught Usman's eye, beyond the aroma of the food, was the indiscreet Welcome Restaurant and Tea Rooms card leaning on the coffee pot. *** *Michelin*.

For the second time Usman, the young mécanicien automobile from Luc-en-Diois, believed he must have arrived in heaven.

Days later, the news of Usman's arrival in the village received much excitement from the younger members of the community, but the complete opposite from its older citizens. They included two of its more, shall we say, marginal inhabitants.

Bran and Branwen Morgan, before their marriage, had taken a vow to live forever on a converted *Cwrwgl*, a Welsh boat made out of woven wood and a waterproof covering. It was moored in the village pond, on a floating dock, directly facing The Duke of Wellington pub. A few days after their wedding, Bran came to a conclusion their living quarters in the small one-person boat had better be enlarged to family size. To his credit, he enlarged the boat. You see, his wife was already eight months pregnant.

During the next two years, Branwen, who had never been ashore since her marriage to Bran, was joined by baby Morgan number two. With that in mind and weighing 113.3 kilos and little exercise, Branwen insisted it was time for them to live onshore. She was fearful her weight would cause the boat to sink and drown them all. Her choice was a waterproof tent in a higher elevation overlooking the pub, in a more upscale neighbourhood.

With their marriage vows to each other broken and their long life dreams in ruin, Bran and Branwen took on a whole new different lifestyle. Bran drank like a fish and smoked pot. Branwen stopped wearing her false teeth, sported the same clothes for months on end and became one of the primary swearers in the village. The rumour was she only ate cheese biscuits as a means, as she put it, to lose weight and return to her pre-marriage slim figure.

Bran, before his marriage to Branwen, had been a very active person, always smiling, in fact probably hyperactive in his formative years. He had been a keen cyclist when younger, but now after moving into their tent-dwelling had an accident on his bike and had to give it up.

One moonless night, after drinking too much beer at The Duke of Wellington, on his way home he became disoriented. His bicycle hit a rock, and he came off his bike with such a thud that Dr Jacobs said Bran had severely fractured his tibia in both of his legs. He would have to stay in bed for weeks. Poor Bran suffered terrible bedsores, his situation deteriorated, bacterial contamination and infection set in. In time he ended up having both legs amputated and died. But, and this is the noblest part of the story, he never stopped smiling.

Usman's next visitor was the Village's full-time business manager extraordinaire, the matronly Miss Gweneth Evans. She arrived, not at Mayor

Hastings' bidding, but to check on the clinic's supplies as well as to get a private peep of Usman, the Usman who spoke Usman.

Miss Evans, as she was called by the villagers, out of respect by all who dared to face her, would have been comfortable being called, 'Sir.' Both Felicity and Penelope were scared stiff of 'Sir.' For underneath that portly figure of no-nonsense was a woman who, in her early twenties, had been called by her middle name Donwen, the Welsh patron saint of lovers. Donwen had found a great deal of the pleasure of offering her infinite and never-ending carnal abilities to many young handsome men of the village, as well as tantalising them with her self-designated title of poet laureate and member of the Welsh Bard. But now, having outlived all of her devotees, she had become resigned, due to old age, to accept Donwen was no more. She, therefore, found great comfort, in her later years, in the pleasure of calling herself Gwenllian Ferch Gruffudd – Princess Consort of Deheubarth. Deheubarth was the only known example of a medieval period woman leading a Welsh army into battle.

Dafyyd Williams, owner and master baker of the Village Bakery, as well as being the village's Conservation and Health & Wellness Council member, was a pleasant, friendly chap. He was small in stature with a magnificent countertenor singing voice that would make a dying Welsh daffodil spring to life. His gift to Usman of freshly baked Bara Brith bread, made with fruit, cold tea and glazed over with honey from the village apiary, brought a sense of familiarity to Felicity and Penelope.

Dafyyd, or as he preferred to be called, Dai, was one of those exceptional men who could actually multi-task. His energy illuminated all those around him. From baking in the middle of the night for his customers to attending the Village Council meetings, Dai was the quintessential man of Little Comely. He was empathetic; he could sing, bake, multi-task and might, some said, be the future Mayor of Little Comely. Might! You see, Dai had an issue. In short, he had his own interpretation of conservation. It went far beyond the conventional definition of the sustainable use of nature by humans. And coupled with Health &

Wellness, it put an enormous pressure on Comely's young, healthy and fertile women to stay clear away from Dai at all costs. ☼

During the ensuing days, Usman took all the comings and goings in his stride. His decision to keep quiet by not uttering a single word had reaped benefits for him, and he was hesitant to change this arrangement. However, the dilemma he faced was he wanted to sustain the patient-nurse relationship as long as possible. Yet, such a mirage of deception was becoming more and more difficult. For his smiles to Felicity and Penelope now included him moving up and down his bushy eyebrows that were quickly translated by the twins into a language they understood.

The twins saw his non-verbal language as a

sign of an impending change in their relationship with him, and they prepared to pounce upon it at the earliest possible occasion.

Owain Jones was a gentle giant through and through. He had the reputation of having the largest feet in the village measuring 29.5 cm. He was a man of considerable character, in his height, a full 1.9 metres. His girth was no different.

Owain presented himself to Usman by the use of sign language – of sorts. Usman got Owain's occupation right, for the most part. After all, what difficulty could arise in explaining, in sign language, the business of being a dentist, a barber or being a butcher? It was when Owain produced a large pig sticker knife from his coat pocket and dramatically pulled it across his own neck that Usman could no longer keep quiet. *"Pour l'amour d'Allah, aidez-moi!"* he screamed, bringing Felicity and Penelope and Dr Jacobs running to his assistance.

Game up!

"No. No-no-no!" responded Owain Jones. "For

goodness' sake, this is what I use to slaughter my pigs. Not kill people!"

And with that, Owain Jones, the dentist, barber, butcher and pig sticker knife owner, made a hasty retreat back to his abattoir.

From his hospital bed, Usman the Usman who spoke Usman realised he had lost the one advantage that had taken him to this point. He glanced at Felicity and Penelope looking for support. The twins would have nothing of it and swiftly turned away from him and went into conference mode as if he didn't exist.

Dear reader, let us pause for a minute and give some thought as to what just happened. Speaking metaphorically, what is coming down the pike? Usman has acknowledged he not only spoke French, but he is of the Muslim faith. Owain, who-could-never-keep-a-secret Jones, has met for the first time, a Muslim. Usman, albeit French-speaking, has entered the sanctity of his beloved Little Comely-on-the-Marsh. As to the twins, Felicity and Penelope, they will probably look for guidance from Dr Moishe Jacobs. Moishe, as we might gather, is the Hebrew name for Moses.

All of this kerfuffle was once again interrupted by a visit of Captain Idris and his beloved Aelwen. Aelwen, arriving for her second dramatic visit to the now-famous Usman was, to put it mildly, full of hot air.

"Yes, Idris, what is it you want?" remarked an exasperated Dr Jacobs.

"It's my left foot. I'm losing sensation in it. It seems to be getting numb."

Dr Jacobs looked at Felicity and then at Aelwen, shook his head, walked backed to his office as he asked Felicity to handle the problem.

"Well Idris, let have a look at it then, shall we? We'll see what we can do for you and Aelwen."

"Ah-ha! I see. Aelwen's right shoe has become entangled in your left shoelace, hasn't? That's what's causing the numbness, isn't it?

Felicity's strong Welsh accent, direct, to the

point when she was annoyed, always ended in typical Welsh fashion by adding a question at the end of a sentence. It was a brutal awakening not unnoticed by Captain Idris or Aelwen. Idris, in his wisdom, felt their time could be better spent elsewhere, probably at The Duke of Wellington having a beer. ☼

The village inhabitants cherished their relationship with each other by acknowledging, but not openly, they must be somewhat unique. Unique? To this, I would go a stage further in saying the vast majority of the residents are, in my opinion, slightly-off-the-wall and need of a profound realignment.

Take, for instance, Harri Thomas, the Village Council member in charge of Parks & Recreation. One cannot get any closer to a real Welshman than our Harri Thomas, the strongest man in the village. He gave up his trade as a master tailor to open the village's only gym. Harri, who was in his 50s, had blue-green eyes, dark hair, rosy cheeks, a short, stocky build and a love for a pint or two of warm beer. Harri acted the part with an infused personality grounded in understanding to all those surrounding him. With one important exception. He never appreciated anyone asking him why he had so much hair growing out of his ears and nose.

In time, and mostly due to the sing-song valleys Welsh accent, Harri Thomas became known to his friends as "Hairy" Thomas.

Hairy was a loveable fellow, willing to help out under any condition, and this is what drove him to volunteer his services to Comely's medical staff.

His arrival caused much-needed relief to Felicity and Penelope. For, if there was one villager who was the nearest to being a normal human being, Hairy Thomas came pretty close to filling the part.

"Hello, girls, if he's," referring to Usman with a wave of his massive hands, "if he's well enough, I can wheel him around the pond to our parks area for a while. He'll be better off for getting some fresh air."

I don't need to be too specific to tell you what Usman thought as he sat in his wheelchair with Hairy Thomas pushing him, at great speed, towards the village pond. A prayer came to mind. *"Rabbi inni zalamtu nafsi faghfirli!"* (My Lord- I have indeed done harm to myself, therefore You protect me!). At the last moment, Hairy steered the wheelchair away from the pond and made a beeline to The Duke of Wellington.

Whatever one might think of Hairy, he was never regarded as the village's executioner. For Usman, a practising Muslim, the choice between drinking alcohol and drowning in a village pond wasn't something he had ever given much thought about. Also, from the way he was tightly gripping the arms of the wheelchair, it became abundantly clear to Hairy his passenger wasn't keen to come in and join him for a pint. In what would seem to be a cooperation of sorts between Hairy and Usman, Hairy saw a simple solution; the outdoor seating area location.

"I'm goin' in, aren't I, to have a pint, or two. I'll get someone to bring you out an orange juice." If in this sentence Usman recognised anything between Hairy's strong Welsh accent and his hand gestures, it was the word 'orange.'

"*Merci beaucoup.*" Seconds later Usman realised he should have kept his mouth closed and just nodded to Hairy. In those two French words, the look of fear on the faces of some of the older villagers sitting outside having a drink said it all.

"Dear God! Have we a foreigner and a French one at that, here with us?" said one woman tightly clasping her two young grandchildren to her breasts. "Hairy, what have you done to us?"

By this time Hairy heard none of the conversation. He had already moved abruptly into The Duke of Wellington, ordered from Mr Wellesley Llewellyn his pint of beer and an orange juice for Usman.

"Here, give me the orange juice, you finish your beer Hairy," remarked the publican. I'll get Blodwin to take it out to the foreigner."

Mr Wellesley Llewellyn, the owner of The Duke of Wellington, was a publican's publican. No doubt about it. As the only pub in the village, he had a standard to keep which was steeped in history. According to Llewellyn, he was related to the Iron Duke through his mother's Irish family, a detail no one ever had any chance of substantiating or questioning. As long as the beer flowed, the villagers could enjoy themselves and socialise, and that was good enough for them.

Wellesley Llewellyn repeatedly told anyone, who would listen, he never went anywhere in public without his dog Kynan. That doesn't mean to say Kynan didn't go anywhere without Llewellyn, for Kynan was a Welsh terrier, with a mind of its own and a fine intelligent character!

If it would be known, the publican never ventured anywhere. He suffered from an anxiety disorder called Agoraphobia. Simply being outside of the pub put him in panic mode.

His condition began in his late teens. There he was, one evening outside the pub, showing off to his mates that he could balance himself on a beer barrel on its side while having a pint of beer in both hands. It was a task he had confidently practised many times. What he didn't know was that Ifor, one of his best pals, had hidden in the same empty barrel waiting to surprise Llewellyn. The story gets depressingly worse. Llewellyn lost his balance and the beer barrel rolled into the pond at its deepest depth. Ifor panicked trying to escape and was hit on the head by a sharp object originating from Bran and Branwen Morgan's converted Welsh boat. He died instantly.

Llewellyn never got over it.

Kynan the Welsh terrier had many friends. One, in particular, was Farch, the moody mare. Kynan and Farch had an extraordinary relationship. Best of buddies. Every day they did their rounds together visiting most of the village's 266 domesticated animals. They all greeted each other as one would a long lost cousin. At precisely at 5:30 in the afternoon, they would wander up to the front gates of the Welcome Restaurant and Tea Rooms hoping to be the recipient of some of chef Meurig ap Griffiths' leftover Pwdin Eva, a baked dessert made with apples and topped with a light vanilla sponge layer.

To return to The Duke of Wellington. Blodwin, the publican's daughter approached Usman with some hesitation. She extended her right hand to offer him a large glass of fresh orange juice while glancing far too long directly into his eyes. It resulted in spilt orange juice all over the front of his legs. Blodwin, with a shriek, and an "Oh my God, look what I've done to you," ran back into the pub for a dry cloth.

This incident, duly noted by many of the ladies sitting outside having their gin and tonics, drove them to immediately want to help their newly-arrived foreigner.

Hairy, by that time, was well into his third pint of beer. And while panic-mode Blodwin looked for a dry cloth, the village ladies, doing their good deed of the day, had encircled Usman in the fascination of meeting a foreigner for the first time. Fortunately, just by chance, Felicity and Penelope passed by and took the situation under their full control.

Returning Usman to the clinic was no mean feat. Usman refused to let go of the arms of the wheelchair, as he had done so a short while ago while in the protective custody of Hairy Thomas. Thankfully, the girls' expert medical knowledge of how to prise Usman's hands from the wheels included giving him a head and back massage. Usman, in the meantime, regretted not being able to endure the curious touching and poking of many of Little Comely's finest married ladies.

Every council member was present: Mayor Norman Hastings, Captain Idris, Owain Jones, Hairy Thomas, Dai Williams and ex–officio Gweneth Evans.

The monthly council meeting of the Village of Little Comely-on-the-Marsh was preceded with the usual positive reviews of their breakfast.

This meeting was held in-camera and dealt with Usman and the circumstances of his arrival in the village. Who was this Usman? Where did he come from? How did he know where to find the village? His family, if he has one, must be worried by now. What were they going to do with him?

It was Mayor Norman Hastings' idea to have the meeting in-camera, an unprecedented decision, according to his colleagues.

"We have to keep our decision to ourselves, at least at this time. The fewer people know we have a foreigner here in the village, the better it will be," he remarked. He added, "Actually, I want you to know it was Mrs Hastings who came up with the in-camera idea."

Owain Jones raised his hand. "Mayor Hastings, Norman, I hate to spoil your one minute of glory, even my Siamese cat, Opal, knows we have a foreigner here."

Dai Williams stood up. "Now tell me something, Owain, how does your bloody cat know that? Who let the cat out of the bag?" The baker realised he'd made an entertaining quip without realising Owain Jones didn't take lightly to any negative comment against his much-loved Opal.

"Now see here, Williams…" Captain Idris in his self-proclaimed position of legal mediator intervened. "Let's keep our focus on the matter in hand."

Hairy Thomas decided it was now his turn to make some retort. "In hand? Don't you mean in foot?" He was, of course, mockingly referring to the Captain's constant companion, Aelwen, the blow-up human-size doll who was sitting very quietly attached to the Captain's left foot, next to Gweneth Evans.

Gweneth Evans sighed, looked directly into Aelwen's eyes while speaking to Captain Idris. "Yes, I've meant to ask you. What the bloody hell is Aelwen doing here at the Village Council's in-camera meeting?"

The words 'bloody' and 'hell' are used with profound consistently in the village. These two words are an integral part of the Welsh language and culture, although, I will add, they may not entirely be pronounced in the same manner as you would.

Bloody, for example, is pronounced 'bluddy' and hell is pronounced without the 'h' as in 'ell.' Together, they form 'bluddy 'ell.' They are the original words used by the Welsh and learned soon after they are born.

Gweneth Evans' caustic comment simply exasperated the situation. The bloody hells continued and the Council Meeting erupted into I-said-you-said-she-said-he-said, resulting in Captain Idris walking out in disgust with his beloved Aelwen.

Mayor Norman Hastings looked around at the empty room. "Well then, I suppose the meeting's adjourned, isn't!" All the other Council members had followed Captain Idris' and Aelwen's lead and were already out of the room. ☼

It was just three weeks since Usman arrived unannounced in Little Comely. He recollected hardly a thing, other than he remembered driving to his grandmother's home in La Motte-Chalançon, sliding off the road and ending up in a ditch.

He wondered if the police had searched for him. The very thought the French police were looking for his remains brought a sneer to his face. The nearest police station to where he lived in Luc-en-Dios was 88 kilometres away in Montélimar.

He imagined, with some pleasure, the local

police searching along route D61 looking for his remains. His remains, Usman, a young Muslim car mechanic originally from Syria. What did they care!

Brought back to reality, his thoughts turned to his loving mother and grandmother, the only two surviving family members of his family.

Usman was generally correct about the search for him. But, what he had underestimated was the empathy of the local communities in Luc-en-Dios and La Motte-Chalançon. For it was they who initiated the investigation while consoling his two family members.

Only Felicity, Penelope and Dr Jacobs knew first-hand the story of how Usman was found lying face down under a large plane tree, several kilometres from the village.

Every Saturday morning Dr Jacobs took it upon himself to take his two nurses into the forest so that they could learn more about savoury as an antiseptic, oregano used against respiratory diseases and rheumatism, and thyme, in the treatment of bronchitis and liver disease. The doctor took immense pride in his knowledge of medicinal plants for the treatment of diseases prevalent in the village.

After assessing Usman's condition, all three of them managed to lug him back to their clinic where they cleaned him up, bandaged him in the Welsh national colours of red, green and white and put him to bed.

The Duke of Wellington pub, with its outside seating arrangement facing Little Comely's pond, had what I would call the winning touch for being in the top 20 of the most beautiful villages in France.

If the exterior of the pub had character, the interior would have put many a history museum to shame. Scores of paintings and illustrations of Arthur Wellesley, 1st Duke of Wellington adorned the walls, as well as maps and military paraphernalia of Wellington's victory against Napoleon at the Battle of Waterloo in 1815. On the left-hand side of the pub's counter, in all its glory, in a gold frame, was a signed daguerreotype of

Wellington by Antoine Claudet.

"That's been in my family for generations," Llewellyn would repeat countless times a day to anyone who would listen. But no one believed him.

The pub, of course, had its regulars who demanded just two things. One, Llewellyn had to have their pint ready for them as they immediately walked into the pub. This was not as difficult as it might seem. For Llewellyn would recognise their voices from 20 metres away. Two, their regular seat was empty at all times. Again, this was never an issue, since all the locals had no hesitation of telling any non-regular whose chair it was they had sat on.

Members of the Village Council had their regular corner, where they met most evenings for a drink. Generally, Hairy Thomas, by far the most prolific drinker of the group, always ordered the first round of beer. He was followed in order, by Dai Williams, Owain Jones, Gweneth Evans, Captain Idris and lastly by Mayor, Norman Hastings. The Mayor was always the last to arrive. He made sure Mildred, his wife, had fallen asleep while knitting before sneaking out of his house for a pint.

Owain Jones cleared his throat. "I remember when I was young my father telling me a story his grandfather had told him, no his great-grandfather, yes I think it was his great-grandfather…"

"For goodness sake, Owain! Get on with the bloody story then!" piped up Dai Williams.

"They found this stranger hanging from a tree in our forest. By all accounts, he must have been hanging there for days."

"Dead was he?" interrupted Captain Idris.

"No, he was just having a bloody nap!" snapped Gweneth Evans.

A lull fell over the group.

"Norman, how's Mrs Hasting's health?" asked Hairy Thomas. "I heard she's been a bit poorly?"

Mayor Hastings replied with a look in his eyes that meant trouble ahead. "Hanging by a rope, you said. In our forest, on a tree?"

Dr Jacobs' health care facility was distinctive in every aspect. It offered a wide range of services, including a small ambulatory surgical centre and a walk-in clinic for the village's community in a clean, spotless environment. On the waiting room wall a sign said, *"Mewn pob daioni y mae gwobr."* (There's reward in every goodness).

The facility also had a small pharmacy and a two-bed section designated for overnight patients where Usman was first brought to on his arrival several weeks ago.

Little Comely's inhabitants were extraordinarily healthy, and Dr Jacobs' flair for medicine provided preventive care, health education to patients and looking after the occasional broken bones.

With Usman's arrival and their first overnight patient in recorded memory, Dr Jacobs and his two nurses had to adjust their daily routine to accommodate Usman. They did so splendidly, although Penelope was somewhat upset she would have to occasionally sacrifice her afternoon Welsh creative arts class decorating many a *Mari Lwyd.*

The *Mari Lwyd* comprises of an artificial horse skull, adorned with stunning decorations, such as coloured ribbons, all fastened to a long pole. Attached to the back of the skull, is a white sheet draped down to hide the individual holding up the pole.

Penelope had, in her mind, become one of the foremost artists of the street graffiti European period. She had eased into it several years ago when caught in the act of drawing a graffiti piece of Mildred Hastings, the Mayor's wife, sitting on a gold toilet seat. If that wasn't enough to create an impression she attached it on the exterior wall of The Duke of Wellington pub, facing the pond.

Her work created quite an interest. Many villagers tried to see the symbolism in the artwork. School children, restricted only to those in the most senior grade, were assigned to write a project about it. Mayor Hastings, who was also the Justice of the Peace, eventually decided he had better charge Penelope with some offence, even though he acknowledged the graffiti, at a specific angle, did resemble his wife. In due course, Penelope was charged and put on probation for one year.

Just by chance, the artistic director of Little Comely's Community Arts & Crafts Centre, had seen Penelope's creative skills and suggested to the Justice of the Peace that she take Penelope under her wing and guide her to a more respected medium of the traditional Welsh art world. Penelope propelled herself into it and eventually produced hundreds of *Mari Lwyds.* They were all used during Little Comely's Annual International Mari Lwyds Festival of Concert, Song, Poetry and Prayer.

The Festival took place on March 1st, St David's Day. It was the highlight of the year for the vast majority of the village population. It was a day of splendid Welsh choir music, mixed with the finest poetry and dance, some dating back hundreds of years. But -there's always a but. There was something exclusive that set Little Comely's festival in a different category to all other celebrations. Some might call it a legendary love story dating back to the laws set down by the ancient druids in the 10th century AD, but with a twist. Instead, as tradition dictated of a white-robed druid climbing an oak tree to cut down mistletoe with a golden sickle, Little Comely's early historians gave a different account. You see, mistletoe and oak trees were not part of the forest ecosystem surrounding the village. So in its place, *Mari Lwyd* came into being as an integral part of the village's annual festival.

The Festival started at 9:00 in the morning. The villagers came down to the village pond, surrounded it with their individual *Mari Lwyds*, and deposited the poles with the horses' skull into the water, which were then pushed out to the centre of the pond. There, one of Little Comely's single young ladies, decked out in her traditional Welsh costume, *Gwisg Gymreig draddodiadol*, would stand up in a Welsh boat waiting to receive the first *Mari Lwyd* of the season. Picking it out of the water and holding it high above her head gave her the right to choose a suitable lover.

Last year, with great enthusiasm, Penelope was chosen for this honoured task. Regrettably, not one *Mari Lwyd* reached her. They all sank. And in a fit of irrational behaviour, she lost her balance, tipped the boat and fell into the water. It was after this incident Penelope decided to focus more on her graffiti artistic ability.

Felicity, as Penelope's sensitive twin sister, was the quieter of the two. She didn't have her sister's flamboyant artsy character. Felicity preferred to remain in the background, doing her work as a nurse with the utmost dedication, an act not unnoticed by Dr Jacobs. She looked forward to their Saturday morning walks in the surrounding forest. She acquired a great interest in learning more about what plants might be used in supplementary medicine.

Her interests as a nurse, more than frequently, meant checking up on the health of their only in-house patient, Usman. By this time neither of them had difficulty in communicating with each other. A smile here and there, an expression through one's hands, and the occasional utterance in their own language was understood. Usman always looked forward to Felicity's hourly visits which became more frequent as the days progressed. A giggle turned into laughter, and the occasional touching each other complemented their behaviour.

During one of the twins Saturday morning walk with Dr Jacobs, the Doctor took Felicity aside. "Remember, he's not one of us. He'll have to return to his people. And Felicity, that day is fast approaching!" ☼

Twm, the Mayor's son, from an early age, was always regarded in the traditional sense, as a little different. Dr Jacobs summed it up in one short, terse sentence to Twm's parents. "Your son is a socially anxious introvert."

To Mildred and Norman Hastings Dr Jacobs' diagnoses came as an utter shock. They thought their darling son, now approaching his 19th birthday, was just shy.

"Perhaps he'll grow out of it. It's probably a stage in his life. I wish he would have more friends his age," Mayor Hastings said to his wife as they walked home.

"Norman, perhaps we should consider getting a second opinion?"

"A second opinion? With who? Are you bloody well mad? Have you forgotten, Jacobs is the only medical Doctor we have in the village?"

"Yes, I know! But, you know what I mean, he's really not one of us, is he, and he doesn't know our culture from way back."

If there was one place Twm felt at home, it was in Dr Jacobs' clinic. He had a regular place where he sat, undisturbed, under the window sill, crossed-legged on the floor, with his back to the gardens. His sole means of communicating was mostly with a nod of his head or a shrug of his shoulders. Conversation on topics such as scientific biblical exegesis, or medieval philosophic theology, to name a few, didn't interest him. To sum up: Twm's personality in one word; "Quirky" would be appropriate!

Directly facing Twm was Usman's bed, now festooned with a selection of dark milk chocolate, seedless red grapes, peaches and mangoes, all from well-wishers of the Little Comely Married Ladies Circle. At a committee meeting, they had decided, by a unanimous vote, to take Usman, if I may use some discretion, to take him under their wing.

It was Usman who took the first step. He gestured Twm to join him to share in the fruit he had received from his admiring ladies. It was an offer Twm could not refuse. Both of them, in perfect harmony, sat in silence as they focused first on the grapes, then the mangoes, the peaches and then the dark chocolate. It reminded me of the movement of a symphony. First, the sonata, followed by the adagio, the minuet and finally the rondo. All in perfect order. Mission accomplished! Twm felt he owed his new-found friend a sign of his gratitude.

What happened after that would in time be written up in the village's historical records. Twm spoke. Not a shrug. Not a facial acknowledgement. Two words. "Thank you!" The significance of the event could be compared to Piotr Ilich Tchaikovsky taking it upon himself to personally fire the five cannon shots in his 1812 Overture.

During the ensuing days, Twm's and Usman's friendship nurtured. With Dr Jacobs' approval, Twm was allowed to take Usman, in his wheelchair, to various highlight spots in the village, where he would attempt to explain the significance of the location. Their language barrier put off neither of them, for it showed, with credible evidence, friendships can overcome such obstacles. For Twm, it meant he had finally found a real friend he could speak to without being discouraged by his parents, who thought him to be dumb and stupid. Usman rallied to the challenge. Twm was not a threat.

Food, as in any friendship, played an essential part in their relationship. Dai Williams' The Bakery was their first stop, followed by Meurig ap Griffiths' Welcome Restaurant and Tea Rooms. But, the best part of the day for Usman was a visit to Owain Jones' Fish and Chip shop. The fact that Owain also ran a barber and butchers shop, and a dental office, all from the same location, didn't seem to faze Usman.

It took no time at all for Mildred Hastings to hear her beloved socially anxious introvert son was gallivanting around the village with the foreigner.

Dr Moishe Jacobs, in the meantime, was quite prepared for the consequences of continuing to treat his only in-house patient. And his preparation couldn't have come at a better time, as a demonstration was at hand.

The bunch of vaudeville protesters, led by Mildred Hastings, included on her left, none other than the widowed Branwen Morgan, Comely's official swearer. On her right, Aelwen, Captain Idris' ever beloved blow-up doll and on Aelwen's right the villages' 12th-century legal expert Captain Idris attempting to keep up with them all. Behind this heterogeneous bunch, the one-eyed Chief Constable Gruffydd, Meurig ap Griffiths, Chef and Owner of Welcome Restaurant and Tea Rooms and nurse Penelope, the village's foremost graffiti artist. She had joined the group on a whim without the faintest idea of knowing where they were heading. All that was missing was a brass band.

In his capacity of being the Mayor and the Justice of the Peace, Mayor Norman Hastings decided to stay behind. It was a prudent decision, and according to members of his Village Council, it was not only the wisest but regarded as the only sensible decision he had ever made in his life. Accordingly, the Village Council voted to take Norman down to The Duke of Wellington for a pint, or two.

Dr Jacobs, Felicity and now rejoined by her out of breath twin sister Penelope, were waiting for them. Wearing N95 respirators and protective clothing they had positioned themselves outside of the main entrance to the clinic. At the same time, Twm and Usman agreed to be safely locked up, in the centre's Intensive Care Unit.

Mildred Hastings and her assorted bunch of oddities came to an abrupt halt some 50 metres away. It was not what they had expected. To use one's creative imagination, I would compare it to a short-toed treecreeper's disappointment in not finding any insects to eat in beech or juniper trees.

By all accounts, it was a Little Comely standoff. In the blue corner: three white gowns, face masked and sterile gloved good guys. And facing them, in the red corner, a large rotund lady flouting a flowered hat and white gloves, who was accompanied by a chef wearing his toque Blanche, white double-breasted jacket, black pants and his customary apron. Behind them stood the one-eyed overweight Chief Constable together with the widow Morgan, the village's all-time official swearer. She was wearing clothes she hadn't washed in months, that complemented her body odour and her refusal to wear her false teeth.

Three pairs of eyes in the red corner turned to look for guidance from law enforcer Chief Constable Gruffydd. "Yes, well," he said with the hesitancy of a Welsh Methodist evangelical revival Christian, attending for the first time, an ultra-orthodox Jewish boy's bar mitzvah. "Ah, yes! I think it would be best if we went on our way." He was totally convinced if they stayed there any longer, they would catch a contagious immunodeficiency disorder.

With that, the three pairs of eyes, plus one, with

their shoulders showing defeat at their lack of leadership, turned around and went home. They were no match for the blue corner, who responded in a most civilised manner.

"Let's go inside and have a nice cup of tea and see how our two guests are coping. They have been locked up far too long in our ICU," remarked Dr Jacobs. "Penelope put the kettle on and let's open the new package of digestive biscuits, the chocolate ones we were saving for a special occasion. There will be more battles ahead. Little Comely just can't handle outsiders."

Felicity, with pride in her eyes at being an integral part of the first demonstration she had witnessed in the village, clearly knew who she supported. Dr Jacobs. Her body language couldn't hide the many questions she had for Dr Jacobs.

"Dr Jacobs, you were once an outsider, but eventually accepted into the community. What do our people have against Usman? "

"Felicity, somethings are very hard to figure out." He paused, took a deep breath and raised his hand as if to say to her, let me continue. "Plato, the ancient Greek philosopher said: 'We can easily forgive a child who is afraid of the dark; the real tragedy of life is when men are afraid of the dark.' You see, our village is isolated from the rest of the world. Our forefathers wanted it this way and, so far, it's been quite a good existence. We're self-sufficient in every way. Of course, we have our fair share of passive lunatics, which make our personal lives, yours and mine, seem almost palatable. Our environment is clean and healthy, and the village is encircled by a forest containing the most incredible foliage imaginable."

Dr Jacobs broke his digestive in half, put one piece in his mouth, sipped on some tea and continued.

"And then comes along this young man Usman. An outsider. He doesn't speak our language. His facial features are different from ours, and his religion is unlike ours, I mean yours and mine. Felicity, do you see where I'm going with this? Do you and Penelope understand? Our community is afraid of him." ☼

All the patrons in The Duke of Wellington couldn't stop talking about it. "So Norman, what's your Mildred been up to?" It was Owain Jones, Little Comely's barber, dentist, butcher, abattoir owner and the village Transportation Manager, who first opened up the subject. They were all there, sitting around the table. Hairy Thomas, from Parks and Recreation; Dai Williams, owner of The Bakery, Conservation, Health & Welfare; Gweneth Evans, Little Comely's full-time Business Manager and Captain Idris, the village's lawyer accompanied by his beloved constant companion Aelwen.

The Mayor, who had to squeeze in to sit beside Aelwen, slowly turned towards all of them, one by one. As his eyes moved around the table, taking time to pause at each of them, he took a long sip of his beer. At the same time, his Council members waited with bated breath for his thought-provoking statement, a statement that would set the village on fire.

It was Aelwen who received the full force of his profound message as he put his face directly inches away from her.

"A man with one watch knows what time it is; a man with two watches is never quite sure. Excuse me!" And with that, Mayor Norman Hastings got up and walked over to the bar to order another round of drinks.

"What the hell is he getting at?" Dai Williams asked as he wiped his bakers' sourdough hands through his hair.

"Beats me. Bloody hell, I haven't a bloody clue!" remarked Hairy Thomas! "Still, who cares? As long as he buys another round of drinks for us!"

All eyes focused on Gweneth Evans, not because of her intellectual ability to explain what the Mayor had said. No! They were all paying attention to her dangling breasts, for the most part, resting on the table in front of them, floating on a pool of leftover beer.

"Look, he doesn't even own a watch!" remarked Hairy Thomas stretching his long legs under the table while inadvertently touching Aelwen's knee. "He doesn't! Ask him what time it is when he comes back with the drinks."

Norman Hastings, the Mayor of Little Comely-on-the-Marsh's 347 Welsh inhabitants, plus 115 cats, 143 dogs, one horse, two pigs, a milking cow and four sheep, returned to the table with a tray of pints of beer for each of his Council colleagues, plus a small mango juice for Aelwen. You see, Norman, out of the clutches of Mildred, his wife, was a decent man at heart. One could say he had empathy towards blow-up sexy dolls not being left out of the conversation. Yes, one could, within a stretch, say that with utter confidence.

It was Gweneth Evans who, after three minutes and already with an empty glass of beer, broke the silence. "Norman, what time is it?" If one could have heard a *Noix de Grenoble* fall onto the pub floor, this would have been the time. For not only did the Village Council member's pause from drinking their beer, but all the chattering of the patrons of The Duke of Wellington ceased. They also all had the itch to hear the Mayor's answer.

Dramatically as it all seems, before the Mayor could open his mouth, all eyes moved away from him to focus on the front door of the pub. Two shadows presented themselves, and in the best thespian tradition, one of the shadows stepped forward and with remarkable deference to Henry Wadsworth Longfellow said:

"Ships that pass in the night, and speak each other in passing, only a signal shown, and a distant voice in the darkness; So on the ocean of life, we pass and speak one another, only a look and a voice, then darkness again and a silence."

"Hi, Dad!"

Wellesley Llewellyn, the publican, responded.

"Bloody hell! It's Twm. He actually spoke for the first time!"

"Hi, Daddy!" Twm entered from the shadows. The smile on his delicate face disregarded everyone, except Norman Hastings, his dad.

"Hi, Daddy? It's me, your son Twm." Twm stepped a little closer to his dad, extended his arms looking for a response. There wasn't any, just a murky cloud and dead silence. ☼

Days later the village was still talking about what happened and the struggle Norman Hastings had in expressing himself to his son. What caused him to entrench his emotions towards Twm? Indeed, nothing could have prepared him hearing his son speak for the first time. Twm needed an outlet in which to express himself, and he selected his dad to be the benefactor. For Twm, when it came to the subtleties of his family, the issues were beset by the conflict between his parents.

As to what exactly happened to Twm while he

and Usman were locked up in Dr Jacobs' ICU remains a mystery. Twm was a physically fragile young man, yet intellectually gifted, who had never spoken to another human.

Deprived of emotional support from his parents, in one afternoon he had blossomed into one of Plateau de Valensole's beautiful early July fields of Lavendula Angustifolia. And all of this was attributed to Usman.

It was a few hours before Twm and Usman returned to Dr Jacobs' clinic. Their disappearance caused quite a fuss. Dr Jacobs had thought of a search party would be in order, led by the one-eyed Chief Constable Gruffydd and Waterloo, the nervous police dog.

But, the concern was all for naught. Blodwin, the publican's buxom daughter, on one of her daily afternoon walks, had spotted them sprawled out on the other side of the village pond eating fish and chips. From the opposite side of the pond she waved at them, hopeful by chance, they would recognise her. She was not disappointed.

With that encouraging sign, she hastily checked her appearance, making sure her mascara wasn't running and walked towards them with a stride of a determined publican's daughter. Her Duke of Wellington baseball cap was firmly on her head and her family's Welsh terrier Kynan was close by her side.

One could say her approach wasn't particularly novel for someone her young age, other than Blodwin had a unique side to her personality. She was known to have a fetishism towards malt vinegar. At an astonishing distance of 25 metres, her ears would start flapping, her nose started sniffing, and her eyes would focus on her objective. Lord help us if anyone was in her way!

It was on this glorious afternoon that in years to come the day would be referred to as *"Blodwin's Day."* With the sun shining directly on her face and her respiratory allergies acting up, her stride towards her destination took on an entirely new energy of life. All thoughts about her dad, Wellesley Llewellyn coping by himself back at the pub, were obliterated from her mind. For now, she whiffed the malt vinegar laying on top of the crunchy chips, accompanied with a spoonful of tartar sauce for the fish, sent young Blodwin in a tizzy! Sadly, within fifteen metres of reaching her objective, she slipped on some Canada Geese poop, fell into the water, and hit her head on a stone and drowned. ☼

Monday morning. Ten o'clock at *Swyddfa'r Crwner*, (The Coroner's Office). They were all there for the inquest, dressed in black, to pay their respects. The Coroner opened the investigation without a post mortem examination. However, he did gain evidence from the two witnesses, Twm and Usman. They stated, under oath, they were having such a grand time together eating their fish and chips, they didn't hear Blodwin approaching them. Now, in the real world beyond Little Comely-on-the-Marsh, one would not hesitate to suggest, with some justification, how this could have happened. When asked that question by the Coroner, Twm and Usman stated they only realised there was a problem when they noticed Kynan, Blodwin's dog, running around in circles with Blodwin's baseball cap in his mouth. By that time, Blodwin, who couldn't swim, wretchedly had sunk in the 3.6 metres depth of the village pond.

With that information, the Coroner instructed himself, as the Doctor, to issue the Medical Certificate of Cause of Death as "by accidental death by drowning."

Now, you might ask if perhaps a conflict of interest had arisen since the Coroner was none other than Dr Jacobs, who issued the Medical Certificate of Cause of Death. Also, Dr Jacobs was the only individual in the village who had a smattering of French and therefore directed himself to act as Usman's translator. However, Dr Jacobs, in true fashion, also exceeded himself splendidly in his multi-professional positions.

In the time-honoured Welsh tradition, the Wake lasted for several nights before the funeral.

Wellesley Llewellyn, Blodwin's dad, insisted the Wake had to be held at The Duke of Wellington. For, not only that was where his daughter had worked, but also in consideration of his Agoraphobia. Everyone agreed. It was the right thing to do, since free beer and sandwiches were planned.

Blodwin's funeral was an affair to remember. She was so young. Penelope was commissioned by the Village Council to create a vibrant graffiti depicting Blodwin's life, a task that even Salvador Dali would have had difficulty accomplishing. And with the utmost enthusiasm, Penelope produced a life-size image of Blodwin dressed as a bottle of her favourite malt vinegar, floating in the pond, with the Latin words magically painted above her. *"Blodwin. Nos memores sumus vestri. Edere in caelis."* (Blodwin. We remember you. Eat in heaven.)

The villagers came to pay their respects to Penelope's work which she had painted over the front door of Owen Jones' Fish and Chip shop. It was, as her father said at the time, gazing at Penelope's masterful work of his daughter, "Yes, my Blodwin, I think she would have liked it!"

From that summer's day onwards, the day became known as *Blodwin's Day*, to be celebrated annually. The villagers would come down to Owen Jones' Fish and Chips shop to pay their reverences to one of their own. And to Owen Jones's credit, he offered all the youngsters a free half-portion of chips sprinkled with, as he called it, *Blodwin's Famous Malt Vinegar*.

Days after Blodwin's funeral, Mildred Hastings suggested her husband call an extraordinary Village Council meeting to discuss Usman, the foreigner. On good authority, she believed Usman had developed an overpowering influence over her beloved son, Twm. "He has to go!" she said with a defiant gesture, raising her pointed index finger and clenched fist towards the side of her head.

"What do you mean, woman, you want to get rid of our son?"

"Of course not, you fool! It's Usman! Norman, take care of it!"

A week later the Village Council, after one of Meurig ap Griffiths' superb breakfast, sat down again to discuss what to do about Usman. Usman by now had become a cause célèbre with many of the village ladies.

"Right, now!" Mayor Norman Hastings set the ball rolling by expressing such a profound statement to his colleagues, who were all a bit shocked at the mayor's aggressive declaration. "Right, now!" typically wasn't part of the mayor's vocabulary. For, if at all possible, he was known to avoid making comments that would have made him look as if he was a prize nincompoop!

"Norman, do you think you can be a little more explicit? What do you mean by '*Right, now?*'" chimed in Hairy Thomas, as he looked around the table for support.

It was Captain Idris, who was about to sacrifice himself again by making the first step in his decent to the netherworld.

"I believe what Mayor Hastings is saying, is that it's time to ask Usman to leave Little Comely-on-the-Marsh. Mayor Hastings, am I correct?"

Most of those sitting around the table weren't the least interested in Mayor Hasting's response. They were more absorbed in what Aelwen, Captain Idris' beloved, was wearing.

Aelwen's outfit, if one might call it that, expressed a daring aesthetic style and approach. It radiated in its creativity and irreverence, putting any design by Nicholas Ghesquièr to shame. One wonders if Ghesquièr would have been able to create such a masterpiece for a life-size blow-up doll. It contained a giant hoop skirt, elaborately designed in rich, vibrant colours of the Welsh flag, interwoven with tiny dragons and leeks.

As to Captain Idris, he had made a third career change in his 89-year-old life, from being a lawyer to a dressing up as WW1 pilot, and now to a fashion evangelist.

It took Gweneth Evans all of her will-power to remain silent throughout what many people would assume as being Captain Idris' magnum opus. I'm sure, if Gweneth had the tenacity to speak the language of the arts, she would have been the first to refer us to the well-known comment attributed to her favourite politician, Sir Winston Churchill to George Bernard Shaw:

"George Bernard Shaw offered Winston Churchill tickets to his play with a note, saying, "Have two tickets for opening night. Bring a friend if you have one." Churchill replied: "Impossible to come to first night. Will come to second night, if you have one."

However, Gweneth's personality did not approach such eloquent lucidity. She responded in the only way she knew how: "Idris, all that is missing from Aelwen's theatrical outfit is a Welsh daffodil attached to her brainless head, accompanied with a large safety pin. Ba-boom!"

And with those words of inspiration, Little Comely-on-the-Marsh's council meeting erupted, once again, into chaos with all of them storming out, with exception to Mayor Hastings who just sat there wondering what had just happened.

It was all very different at Dr Jacobs' clinic. Patients were sitting peacefully in the waiting room, chatting to each other and biding their time to be called into the doctor's office by nurse Felicity or Penelope. Usman and Twm were there having decided, with Dr Jacobs permission, to set up a temporary space in the corner of one of the examining rooms. They had become inseparable, spending as much time together as they could. Usman had taken to teaching French to Twm, who readily accepted the task.

Both Felicity and Penelope had made a 'play' for Usman during his first weeks in the village. But now they had resigned themselves to accepting the relationship between Usman and Twm had taken on a different meaning.

Felicity had taken it quite badly. She had been quite sure Usman favoured her. As to Penelope, well, she had realized her artistic ability had given her a new meaning of life as the Village of Little Comely-on-the-Marsh's designated Artist in Residence.

Dr Moishe Jacobs was so taken by her artistic ability, he gave her the commission to paint his waiting room, but with a proviso. He said, with a smile on his face, only light blue and white were to be the colours she should use. Also, the theme should depict, with political overtones, an artist's interpretation of a calm, relaxed medical facility.

Penelope gladly accepted the commission. Through her previous rejected artworks, she had gradually understood what it meant to be utterly disliked as an artist by the Village Council. This was her opportunity to show them her creative talent never before achieved by anyone.

Felicity broke the news to Dr Jacobs. At the time he was on one of his regular Saturday morning walks in the forest looking for various medicinal plants for the treatment of diseases prevalent in the village population.

"Ah Felicity, I'm happy to see you. Come and have a look at my Ganoderma lingzhi!" Dr Jacobs was, of course, referring to his newfound friend, commonly referred to as 'the King of mushrooms', recognised by some to prevent or treat various diseases.

Felicity was in no mood to see the Doctor's Ganoderma lingzhi, or anything else he wanted to show her. She immediately explained to him her sister's latest creative work and by all accounts, probably her last.

By the time they arrived back at the clinic, Penelope was waiting for them. Indeed, Penelope had painted the waiting room in light blue and white. That was a given. Regrettably, she had described her interpretation of a calm, relaxed medical clinic far beyond the boundaries of politics and tranquility.

Penelope's theme, as she enthusiastically explained to her client, was based, nay loosely based, upon the painting by Lord Frederic Leighton's *Actaea, the Nymph of the Shore*. One may remember, in Greek folklore Actaea was a sea nymph who helped sailors on their journeys when they faced severe storms. In Leighton's painted work, Actaea is spread out in the frontal nude position, in the sand, watching her dolphin friends from the shore. Nurse Penelope, Little Comely-on-the-Marsh's Artist in Residence, had taken Leighton's Greek mythology painting one step further. She portrayed herself as Actaea and her dolphin friends as members of the Village Council, frolicking nude in the water.

Penelope looked at the Doctor. "Dr Jacobs, painting from nature, is not copying the object; it realises one's sensations." She paused, and as she walked out of the waiting room with a smug look on her face, she turned to both Dr Jacobs and her sister and said, "Paul Cézanne said that!"

Felicity turned towards Dr Jacobs. "I think I'll put the kettle on for a nice cup of tea."

One could hear, in the forest background, Little Bustards and Pin-tailed Sandgrouse's singing as Dr Jacobs and nurse Felicity sat in perfect silence, looking at each other while drinking their nice cup of tea, accompanied with the occasional crunch of a digestive biscuit.

Dr Jacobs broke the silence. "Felicity, do you think you could possibly go and find Usman and Twm for me?"

Twm spoke first, while Usman couldn't help staring at Penelope's self-portrayal of Actaea.

"Bloody hell, is this what's she's been up to then?"

"Lads, I need you to cover up and paint over Penelope's work by this time tomorrow. That will give the paint enough time to dry before I see my first patient on Monday morning, who is..?" Dr Jacobs turned towards Felicity.

"Your mother, Twm, the mayor's wife, Mildred Hastings, at nine o'clock."

After three coats of paint and twelve hours later, the task set out by Dr Jacobs was accomplished! The waiting room had been re-painted in light blue and white. ☼

The 347 inhabitants of Little Comely-on-the-Marsh were avid domestic animal lovers. Dai Williams, the village's Conservation, Health & Wellness Council member accepted the task of conducting a door-to-door census of the cat and dog population. Weeks later he proudly announced there were 115 cats and 143 dogs. Added to the census were one horse, two pigs, a milking cow and four sheep. In essence, every household had both a cat and a dog. What was so extraordinary and I'm sure purely coincidental, was all the cats had the same name, Siam and most of them were all grey tabby cats. The rumour, as Dai Williams explained to his colleagues; the cats were all descendants from the time the Roman army in the south of France brought them from other parts of their Empire to protect their food stock from rats. In time, the Romans departed, and the cats remained.

If there was one pertinent point, according to the minutes of the meeting, it was the statement made by Captain Idris. "If any of those bloody cats think they can use my beloved Aelwen as a scratching post, they're bloody-well are in for a bloody big surprise!" On this occasion there was unanimity between all those present.

Dai Williams, after his awe-inspiring cat report to his colleagues, was promoted from Animal Census Taker to Little Comely's Director, Census Bureau (DCB). As to the dog census, it was a different matter. Dai had never admitted he suffered from an unusual allergic reaction to dogs. Irritant Contact Dermatitis, which, although frequently occurs in dogs, seemed at an early stage in his own life, to find its way to him.

Dai Williams, when he was a youngster, loved to play with the village dogs. He would run with them on his hands and feet, and lay on his back with his feet and hands in the air doing all sorts of naughty doggie things!

At eight years of age, his parents noticed he had acquired the first signs of blister-like lesions on the back of his hands, stomach and lips. The affected locations were very red, and he continually rubbed his feet. Other than a cool, wet compress, or soaking in a cold bath, nothing seemed to work. And that's how it continued throughout his formative years until his parents concluded it would be appropriate to get rid of their dog! However, Little Comely wasn't a typical village, so they kept their son's condition to themselves.

It wasn't until Dai had been appointed as the village's official Animal Census Taker and subsequently Director of Census Bureau, these circumstances came to light. He had visited households wearing nitrile gloves, safety glasses and an N95 respirator.

I'm not exactly sure who became stressed first, the dog or its owner. But it did lead Dai to become known in village households as, "That old DCB!"

He eventually found out it didn't relate to his title, but a more meaningful expression. "Don't Come Back!" ☼

Precisely at nine o'clock, not one minute later, on Monday morning Mildred Hastings, the wife of Mayor Norman Hastings, arrived for her doctor's appointment and immediately noticed the waiting room's freshly painted colours. "Oh my, you have been busy!" she said to nurse Felicity as if implying Felicity had a hand in the work, which wasn't far from the truth. "Light blue and white have such a soothing expression of taste for a doctor's office, don't .you think so? Felicity, do you know why Dr Jacobs choose these colours?"

"Because, how shall I put it, they're my family colours, Mrs Hastings. Now, shall we go into my office?"

"Ah yes, I completely understand," she replied –which she didn't!

"Dr Jacobs, did you know when my Twm was a youngster, bless him, he loved to paint walls."

"Really, Mrs Hastings! How fascinating." With that, Dr Jacobs closed the door behind his patient as he heard Felicity's cup of tea crash to the floor.

That same evening, Penelope was to take over from Felicity's shift and herein lies the problem for Dr Jacobs. After all, he did commission Little Comely's Artist-in-Residence to paint his waiting room, and in her mind, she did. But now..!

Felicity came to the rescue. "Dr Jacobs, Mrs Angharad, the village Head Teacher, is already 40 weeks into her pregnancy. I know she loves Penelope's creative talent. Perhaps when you visit her tomorrow, you can suggest our Penelope might be persuaded to paint something for her, you know, in celebration of the birth."

And that is what happened. Before Penelope arrived for work, Felicity waylaid her coming up the path to the clinic. She told her a cock and bull story that would have indeed won first prize at the *Gŵyl Chwedleua Ryngwladol Cymru*, Wales' International Storytelling Festival. You might ask what colourful tale Felicity told her. Well, of course, I wasn't entirely privy to their conversation; however, Penelope couldn't stop hugging her sister in outright gratitude that must have seemed utterly perplexing to Dr Jacobs.

"Dr Jacobs, oh thank you, thank you, thank you! You are absolute, without question, the kindest, sweetest, incredibalist, thoughtfulist, and consideralist person on the whole planet!" To which Dr Jacobs took it all in stride, not having a clue as to what Felicity had told her sister.

Felicity, as she was leaving the clinic, stopped half-way out of the main door, and turned to Dr Jacobs. "Well, Dr Jacobs, I'm off! That's my shift completed for the day. You're now in the capable hands of Penelope, Little Comely-on-the Marsh's graffiti expert and Artist-in-Residence." And with a smile on her face, she added, *"Ad Me'ah V'esrim*

Shana!"

To this day it remains a mystery as to how Felicity, Little Comely-on-the-Marsh's very own talented nurse, in an outburst of utter self-confidence, offered Dr Moishe Jacobs the Hebrew blessing for longevity and a full life: May you live to be 120 years!

To return to Twm and his friend Usman. It was early Monday morning, vegetable market day in the village. Many stall owners were still setting up their produce and goods which faced The Duke of Wellington pub. It had always been that way. After all, irrespective to the time of day, what better reason could one find than to buy one's fresh veggies followed by drinking a pint of warm beer.

A few stall owners who had arrived at the crack of dawn, were already selling their home-grown vegetables to the early birds, including Twm and Usman. Usman hadn't fully recuperated from his car accident, and he was occasionally still confined to his wheelchair. And so he was that day, with his friend Twm who made sure he kept full control of the wheelchair while avoiding villagers and their dogs.

Over the past weeks, Usman had taken great pains, with the support of Twm and Felicity to attempt to speak English, or as his friends teased him, more like Franglais. His enunciation though was another matter. A Levantine Lebanese-Alawite Syrian Arabic, add that to provençal French, stretched one's imagination to the extreme. However, for the ordinary basic, down-to-earth ladies of the village, it was down-right bloody sexy!

As to Welsh? It was thought Usman would be best to leave it alone. However, he did pick up one expression he couldn't resist repeating at the most inopportune times. *"Yach-a-fi!"* (Yuck!).

Twm tried his best to set some ground rules for Usman, especially at the market, such as don't say it when pointing at the vegetables, or in passing an overweight person, or God forbid at someone's baby child. As Twm put it to Usman: "If you continue, I will not be able to guarantee you'll be breathing at the end of the day!"

The same afternoon, at the insistence of Mildred Hastings, Mayor Norman Hastings, called for an informal lunch meeting of the Village Council regarding Usman, the Usman who spoke Usman. This time it took place at the Welcome Restaurant & Tea Rooms. Much to the surprise of the Village Council, Mayor Hastings invited Chief Constable Gruffydd and his dog Waterloo, who patiently sat outside.

Lunch, and a bloody fine one, consisted of Cawl cennin, a traditional leek and potato soup, seasoned with black pepper and served with a spoonful of cream and crusty bread spread with salted butter. Roast lamb with laver sauce followed it, and for dessert, Welsh Amber pudding served warm with cream. A delicious cup of kopi luwak coffee added to the meal.

"We need a plan of action," remarked Mayor Hastings as his colleagues were still consuming their second helping of dessert. "We need an EP," he added.

"Norman, what the bloody hell is an EP?" All eyes turned towards Hairy Thomas.

"Oh, I know what that is!" said Gweneth Evans, Little Comely's Business Manager. "It's an entry point. I would say it's most crucial, likely to give us the advantage."

"For Christ's sake, what advantage do we need? Aren't we the Village Council? Let's vote on Chief Constable Gruffydd getting on with it and doing his stuff. I've got to get back to my bakery by five this afternoon," said Dai Williams.

"Do you mind if I say something?" It was Captain Idris. He looked with a loving smile at his beloved Aelwen. There was a groan from all those present as if to say, here we go again!

Idris paused, took off his WWI pilot's leather hat and goggles and cleared his throat.

"It's not a simple matter as you think. It's quite complex. Legally, of course, I am not an expert on deportation matters, but has this man Usman conspired to commit a crime or fraudulent act while here? Is he, in fact, a French citizen? Who is he? Where was he born? And how did he arrive here and why? Has he claimed refugee status? Has he asked us for protection? Has he?"

"For goodness sake, Idris! Enough!" None of us here are interested in your legal definitions and questions. You seem to want to slow down the whole process. Whose side are you on? We just want to get rid of the foreigner. He's making himself at home wandering around with Twm. All the village women are attracted to Usman, and he's sure not one of us, is he."

"Hold on a minute! What do you mean by wandering around with my son Twm? When did this start happening?" said an agitated Mayor Norman Hastings.

It was left to Owain Jones to respond gently.

"Oh Norman, you just don't get it. You're getting forgetful. You just don't know what's happening in the village, let alone with your family, do you?"

Mayor Hastings sat there, shook his head, and sighed. "Life, for me, seems so utterly discombobulated." He looked at Gweneth Evans. "Gweneth, please take over running the meeting, I'm going out for some fresh air."

Bloody hell, that's never happened before," remarked Hairy Thomas. He paused and looked at his colleagues. "I've never heard him use big words such as discombobulated! Where did that come from?"

During all this time, the one-eyed Chief Constable Gruffydd sat there quietly observing the situation. He was, after all, the principal police officer in the village, let alone the only one. His motto, clearly defined above the door to his police station-come-home, said it all. *"Acta non verba."* (Action, not words).

Policing had been in his family for generations, and as did his father, he thrived on it. However, there were some apparent differences. His father was much brighter, and an all-round decent human being who the community respected. Besides, he rarely went to church and wanted very little to do with religion, until near his death. Whereas his son, the current chief constable was, how shall I put it? He had some loose ends? That was not all. Religion played an essential part in Chief Constable Gruffydd's life, he wasn't disposed to anyone who, let me say candidly, who didn't follow the traditions of the Welsh Methodist evangelical revival Christian faith. If there was one individual who would thrive on getting this job done, all fingers pointed to Chief Constable Gruffydd. He had, after all, failed once before, for sure it wasn't going to happen again! And as he had said numerous times to Waterloo, his police dog. "Two is two too many!"

Somewhat flustered, Mayor Hastings returned to the meeting shaken up at hearing there was something allegedly going on between his son and Usman.

"What have I missed? Anything I should know about?"

Gweneth Evans offered an answer. "Actually, nothing at all, Norman. We were just talking about our delicious lunch."

All eyes returned to Captain Idris, who was fiddling around with his shoelace that joined him to his beloved Aelwen.

"Well, Idris, what have you to say? Out with it!

Do we have any legal grounds to get rid of him?" remarked Owain Jones, to which Idris just quietly sat there, uncommitted to making a response, while looking down at his empty dessert bowl that had contained two servings of Welsh Amber pudding.

"Hold on a minute, Owen! What do you mean by, to get rid of him?" asked Hairy Thomas.

Hairy's comment was all it took for another emotional outburst to happen. This resulted in Chief Constable Gruffydd excusing himself by making a hasty retreat back to his police station, accompanied by his dog Waterloo. ☼

The Village School, or as the locals knew it, *Ysgol y Pentref*, backed on to the home of Mrs Nala Angharad-Snomis, the school's headteacher. Everyone in the community respected her. Every person simply called her Mrs Angharad, for her name dated back to the twelfth century. Angharad was the wife of Gruffudd ap Cynan, king of Gwynedd. He became revered as King of all Wales, and a significant figure in Welsh resistance to Norman rule. This story in itself, relating to the demise of anything purporting to be French, was enough to put Mrs Angharad on a pedestal.

However, Mrs Angharad, now on maternity leave, was well past her due date, and Dr Jacobs was becoming somewhat concerned. Inducing labour might be the best option.

It was Penelope who resolved the problem. As per her agreement with Dr Jacobs and Mrs Angharad, she had created one of her artistic masterpieces in celebration of the future birth. Her work surrounded the outside door frame of Mrs Angharad's front door. No one could deny the result was extraordinary visual in concept. So much so, the first and only time Mrs Angharad saw it, her water broke, and she immediately went into labour. Penelope called her work, *"The Delivery of the Placenta."* It was the last commission she received as Little Comely's Artist-in-Residence before returning to full-time nursing.

Later that week, Dr Jacobs sat down for a chat with Felicity, Twm and Usman. It took place, in the clinic.

"Usman, I'm giving you a clean bill of health. It's time for you to return to your family in the real world. They must be anxious about you."

"I'm going with him!" Twm had no hesitation in his voice. He was darn well resolute.

Dr Jacobs chose his next words carefully. "Twm, you cannot! I don't mean you cannot in the sense of being forbidden, but Usman's world is so vastly different to our community here.

"There's a Talmudic parable about a rabbi who was once passing through a field where he saw a very old man planting an oak tree. He asked the old man why was he planting the tree, for indeed he didn't expect to live long enough to see the acorn growing into an oak tree.

"The old man looked at the rabbi and said his ancestors planted trees, not for themselves, but us, in order we might enjoy their shade or fruit. And now I am doing likewise for those who will come after me."

Dr Jacobs stood up and put his hand on Twm's shoulder. "You are the future of Little Comely, Twm, together with Felicity and Penelope. Who will plant the trees for future generations if you leave us?"

The Doctor pointed outside, past the clinic, past the trees, past the path to the forest where Usman was found injured, face down, under a large plane tree several kilometres from the village. It was here on Saturday mornings he, Felicity and Penelope looked for medicinal plants for the treatment of diseases prevalent only in the village.

"Twm, you have your way. Usman has his way. As for the right way, the correct way, and the only way, it does not exist for you other than here, in the Village of Little Comely-on-the-Marsh." ☼

To quote Catherine Zeta-Jones, the Welsh actress: "In Wales it's brilliant. I go to the pub and see everybody who I went to school with. And everybody goes 'So what you doing now?' And I go, 'Oh, I'm doing a film with Antonio Banderas and Anthony Hopkins.' And they go, 'Ooh, good.' And that's it."

My grandfather used to take me to his pub, the local as he called it. To him, it was his social centre. I must have been around ten years old at the time. The adventure was supposed to be a secret. "I'm just taking sonny boy, (that's what he called me), for a walk while he's visiting us. We won't be too long!" he would say to me with a wink. As if my grandmother didn't know! Well, we would head down the hill, at a rapidly increasing speed, to his local where I had to sit outside on the bench while he went inside to order an orange juice for me. Other than getting the juice and hastily returning to his friends, I was left alone for at least an hour with a pre-selected bunch of comics to read. Our return to my grandparents' home was somewhat slower than our arrival at the pub.

The Duke of Wellington contained the same trappings as my grandfather's pub. In essence, it was the community's centre of social activity. It formed an essential part of life in Little Comely-on-the-Marsh. After the unfortunate drowning of Blodwin, the publican's daughter, the pub for a while became a more subdued establishment. It lost its centre of energy. Also, the beer for many of its patrons, other than for Hairy Thomas, didn't taste the same.

Mr Wellesley Llewellyn's dog Kynan no longer had anyone to take him for his daily walks.

Llewellyn did make an effort, but he had Agoraphobia, and the very thought of stepping out of the pub gave him anxiety attacks.

Finally, it was left to the widow Branwen Morgan to make the suggestion she had a few spare hours in the afternoon to help out. Mr Wellesley Llewellyn gave it some careful consideration and agreed. He also needed a barmaid to replace Blodwin. But he insisted Branwen put her false teeth back in her mouth, regularly change her clothes and cease swearing at everyone before she could work part-time behind the bar serving his patrons. Branwen Morgan readily agreed.

After a few weeks, the pub returned to its near everyday life. The beer tasted better than ever. Branwen Morgan kept her promises and Kynan, the dog, delighted in going for his walks with her where he met up with his friend Farch, the moody mare. Also, members of the Village Council, at their regular Friday night pub table and now with the inclusion of Chief Constable Gruffydd, continued their heated discussion about what to do about Usman.

It was Captain Idris who initiated the first remark. "As I've already said, the situation is somewhat legally complex and ..." Gweneth Evans smiled, put her hand on Idris' arm. "For goodness sake, Idris! You're talking as if you're one of those egotistical politicians who don't know the answer to a question. We're all friends here, aren't we?"

Chief Constable Gruffydd snorted as a sign he had something to say. "Well, what is it Gruffydd? Out with it, man!" said Mayor Hastings.

"Thank you, sir! I was just wondering what Jesus would do under the circumstances."

"*Jesus?*" The response came in unison.

"Bloody hell Gruffydd! For God's sake, why are you bringing religion into it?" said Owen Jones. "Anyone want another beer? My round!"

By the time Owen Jones had returned with the drinks, one could have cut the air with a knife! "What on earth is going on? You all look so sullen. Did I miss anything?"

Hairy Thomas reached out for his beer. "Sure, you did! Just look around the table. We're supposed to be the leaders in our community. We're nothing but a bunch of bloody weak-kneed crackpots!"

He slowly pointed at everyone around the table. "Look at our Norman Hastings, The Mayor. His wife, Mildred, puts him down on every occasion so that he has difficulty making decisions. Our Business Manager, Gweneth Evans, most people are scared stiff of her. Gweneth, what name do you enjoy being called? Isn't Gwenllian Ferch Gruffudd – Princess Consort of Deheubarth, the only known example of a medieval period woman leading a Welsh army into battle? And then there's you Owain Jones our all-round barber, dentist, butcher, abattoir owner and the Village Transportation Manager. Usman thought you were going to kill him with your pig sticker knife and recently didn't you mentioned something about how can we get rid of him?"

He turned towards Captain Idris, shook his head and snickered. "I've never figured out anything worthwhile about you. You're just a pathetic comic figure following in the footsteps of Hershele Ostropoler, the Jew!"

Hairy's final blow was to Dai Williams, in charge of Health and Wellness. "We all know why our daughters stay away from you, don't we!"

On another occasion, the twenty seconds of silence that followed would have reminded many of the pub's patrons of the well-known quote attributed to Benjamin Disraeli: "Silence is the mother of truth."

However, it was Captain Idris, the very deaf 89-year-old court jester figure, who saved the day. This man, with one of the best legal minds in the village, did something no one in their right mind would have thought of. He picked up one of the pub's forks, and after several attempts, he extinguished the life of Aelwen, his beloved blow-up doll.

Mr Wellesley Llewellyn credited Captain Idris of saving his pub from total carnage. And the Captain's colleagues were in such a state of unbelievable shock at the action he took; they meekly walked out of the establishment and went home.

Later that evening, Dr Jacobs shared his plan with Felicity, the one he had devised to spirit Usman home to his family.

On Saturday morning, at seven-thirty, she was to bring Usman to the spot in the forest where they regularly looked for plants used in the treatment of the villager's ailments. He would meet her there. Felicity looked at him. "And what if Twm wants to join Usman?" Dr Jacobs smiled softly and put his hand on her head. "Then my dear, it will be so. I'm sorry!" ☼

Saturday morning. Twm did join Usman and Felicity, and one could see the grief on her face as the three approached Dr Jacobs. However, the look of despair turned to one of bewilderment the closer the three got to the Doctor. For Dr Jacobs was talking to another man they didn't recognise.

"Felicity, Twm, Usman, I believe you may know this man."

"You may know him as Captain Idris. I know him by his real name. Isaac.

Isaac approached the three, his hand extended. "Shalom, my young friends. Did I surprise you?" He was hardly recognizable. Gone was his court jester appearance, his beloved Aelwen was no more, nor the mockery he was subjected to from his Village Council colleagues.

It was Usman who first stepped forward. *"Assalamu alaykum*, my friend. Peace be upon you!"

Dr Jacobs turned to Usman and Twm. "Isaac will be joining you. Follow him, and he will lead you to where you, Usman, had your car accident on route D61. After that, Isaac will leave you both and take a different route to his family's home."

Twm turned towards the Doctor. "But Dr Jacobs, I'm not going with Usman. I'm going to stay here, with Felicity that is if she agrees."

It was it seems not only a surprise to the Doctor, but also to dear Felicity. She simply couldn't control her emotions, for she had assumed Twm and Usman were not just good friends.

"Now, it's time for our goodbyes," remarked Dr Jacobs. He approached Isaac, hugged him and asked him to give his best wishes to the family. "Shalom, my friend. *Biz hundert un tsvantsig!"* (May you live to be 120 years old!)

Felicity looked at Dr Jacobs. He grinned. "Genesis 6:3: 'And the Lord said: My spirit shall not abide in man forever, for that he also is flesh; therefore shall his days be a hundred and twenty years.'"

Usman turned to face them all. "You are my brothers and sisters. *Shukraan jazilaan lak ealaa musaeadatik."* (Thank you very much for your help).

The walk back to the Village of Little Comely-on-the-Marsh for most of the time was drowned in silence until Felicity couldn't keep quiet any longer.

"Dr Jacobs, I'm bursting. I have so many questions to ask you and…"

He raised his hand. "All in good time Felicity. We'll make time for sure. I promise. In the meantime this afternoon, who have I got coming in to see me?"

Felicity turned to Twm, holding his hand very tightly and with a tight-lipped smile on her face said, "Oh, yes, Doctor! Mildred Hastings wants to see you again about her son!" ☼

.

ABOUT THE AUTHOR

Alan L. Simons was born and educated in London, England. He worked for various newspapers in England before immigrating to Canada where he resumed his career in the newspaper and magazine fields and established a communications company. Currently he publishes an online international news service, now in its 15th year, dealing with issues relating to intolerance, hate, antisemitism, Islamophobia, conflict and terrorism. As a diplomat, he served as the Honorary Consul of the Republic of Rwanda to Canada, post genocide era. He is currently working on his fifth book, *The Children of the Forest,* a children's fairy-tale in the European tradition. The story weaves around the lives of two children who begin a relationship lasting throughout their lives together with five enchanted characters, who live with disabilities.

https://alanlsimons.wordpress.com

baronelbooks@prrotonmail.com

Books by Alan L. Simons

EIGHTEEN MONTHS-A LOVE STORY INTERRUPTED
A story of a human relationship that testifies to the strength and will of both the terminally ill patient and her partner as he comes to accept her illness and the short period of time they will spend together.

THE INCREDIBLE ADVENTURES OF CAPTAIN MACDUDDYFUNK IN CUGGERMUGGERLAND
The children of Canada's Minister of Missing Islands, are magically transported to the mysterious island of Cuggermuggerland where they meet the Quidnuncs, who love to hug and the Shilpits, who always scream and shout at each other.

SWEATY CATS AND BABY PIGEONS
A series of short stories written for the inquiring mind of a young child, in which grandparents can interact and stimulate communication between the generations.

THE VILLAGE OF LITTLE COMELY-ON-THE-MARSH
A hilarious story addressing cultural, diversity and religious concerns, all wrapped up in a bizarre romantic slant that goes beyond the stereotypes of British and French society in today's world.

THE CHILDREN OF THE FOREST (Winter 2020/21)
A children's fairy-tale in the European tradition. Two children begin a relationship lasting throughout their lives together with five enchanted characters, who live with disabilities.

https://alanlsimons.wordpress.com/

Made in United States
North Haven, CT
10 November 2025

82219646R00076